OWEN FOOTE,
MONEY MAN

OWEN FOOTE, MONEY MAN

by STEPHANIE GREENE
Illustrated by MARTHA WESTON

Clarion Books • New York

Clarion Books
a Houghton Mifflin Company imprint
215 Park Avenue South, New York, NY 10003
Text copyright © 2000 by Stephanie Greene
Illustrations copyright © 2000 by Martha Weston

The illustrations for this book were executed in pencil.
The text was set in 14-point Palatino.

www.hmco.com/trade

Printed in the U.S.A.

Library of Congress Cataloging-in-Publication Data

Greene, Stephanie.
Owen Foote, money man / by Stephanie Greene ; illustrated by Martha Weston.
p. cm.
Summary: Ingenious eight-year-old Owen wants to make money for the
things he absolutely needs, such as plastic vomit, but he tries to come up with some
alternatives to earning an allowance, which sounds like too much work.
ISBN 0-618-02369-0
[1. Work—Fiction. 2. Moneymaking projects—Fiction. 3. Family life—Fiction.]
I. Weston, Martha, ill. II. Title.
PZ7.G8434 Ov 2000
[Fic]—dc21   00-027716

MV 10 9 8 7 6 5 4 3 2 1

To Nora, Sophie, and Luke,
who have always loved money
—S. G.

For Niko and Kia,
who dream up great money-making schemes
—M. W.

CONTENTS

FREE TOILET DEMONSTRATION

"Toilet demonstration! Free toilet demonstration!"

Owen stood at the bottom of the stairs in his white lab coat and listened for the sound of stampeding feet.

It was quiet.

"Hey, Lydia," he yelled. He ran up the stairs and knocked on her bedroom door. "Want to watch a toilet demonstration?"

The door opened. Lydia was lying on the floor, surrounded by magazines. Her best friend, Kate Powell, had her hand on the doorknob.

"Yeah, right, Owen," Lydia said in a bored voice. "What are you, demented?"

Ever since Lydia had started middle school, she treated Owen as if he were a baby. Things he did that she used to like, she suddenly hated.

Usually it made him mad. But right now he needed an audience.

"It's free," he said enticingly.

"What do you do in a toilet demonstration?" Kate said. "Show us how to flush?"

Kate liked Owen. She didn't have a brother. Just two older sisters. She had told Lydia she thought Owen was adorable.

"Weird, but adorable, was what she really said," Lydia had told him. "That's all *she* knows." Owen didn't mind "weird," but "adorable" made him gag.

Now he gave Kate a huge fake smile and grabbed her arm.

"I'm glad you asked," he said. He started to lead her firmly toward the stairs. "It's really very interesting, how a toilet works. Most people don't pay any attention to their toilets, but they should."

"Owen, let her go!" Lydia shouted from her room. Then, "Kate!"

Owen kept a firm grip on Kate's arm. By the time Lydia came pounding down the stairs after them, they were halfway through the kitchen.

"It's based on a very simple principle that hasn't changed much since the first toilet was invented," Owen was saying. He was trying to talk in the scholarly voice they used in museums. He wasn't sure of all his facts, but he knew they would sound truer if he said them in the right voice.

That's what grownups did. Grownups didn't always look as if they knew what they were talking about. But the way they said things, in such loud, firm voices, made everyone believe them.

Anyway, right now Owen was pretty sure he knew a lot more about toilets than Kate and Lydia.

He had been studying them for his whole life practically. Ever since he was little, he'd been taking the top off the toilet tank whenever he flushed so he could watch what happened.

When he had first looked inside the tank, it was pretty disgusting. The sides were dark red because of all the iron in the water. And there was a thin line of soft scummy stuff around the edges.

But Owen had been too busy watching to care. He loved the way it worked. It was so simple.

There were no motors, no wires, nothing. Just two rods. The one attached to the handle had a chain at its end. At the end of the chain was a large rubber stopper that rested on the bottom of the tank.

The other rod had a white plastic ball on it that floated on the top of the water.

When Owen pushed down on the handle, it made the rod connected to it rise up. The rod pulled the chain up with it, which lifted the rubber stopper off the bottom.

When the stopper lifted, it uncovered a hole in the bottom of the tank. This was the pipe where the water drained out. As soon as the hole was uncovered, the water rushed out, the level in the tank dropped, and the floating ball dropped with it.

Then the stopper plopped back over the hole, the tank began to fill again, and the floating ball slowly rose back to its original position.

The second it got back to where it had started, everything stopped. The water, the noise, everything.

The sudden silence was the part Owen liked best.

It meant the job was over. The toilet was ready for another flush. Owen didn't know why he found the process so interesting, but he did.

"Right this way, please," he said, steering Kate into the small bathroom off the kitchen. "Mind the step."

"What step?" Lydia said. "This is ridiculous."

Kate laughed. "This is what I meant by weird," she said to Lydia over her shoulder.

"Step right in. There's plenty of room for everyone," said Owen. He waited until Kate and Lydia were both standing in front of him. Then he put his hand on the top of the tank.

"Can everyone see?"

"You'd better get this over with, Owen," Lydia said through clenched teeth. "I mean it."

Owen ignored her. "First things first," he said. He cleared his throat. "Does anyone know who invented the toilet?"

He put an encouraging expression on his face and looked around the tiny bathroom the way teachers did when they were waiting for a show of hands. He made sure not to meet Lydia's eyes.

"Oh, sure, Owen," Lydia snorted. "That's one of those vital facts everyone knows."

"Mr. Flusher?" said Kate. She was smiling, as if she was actually enjoying herself.

"Good guess," Owen said. "Anyone else?"

"There *is* no one else," said Lydia.

From the tone of her voice, Owen could tell he didn't have much time left. "It was Thomas Crapper," he said quickly, "more than a hundred years ago."

"Thomas Crapper?" said Kate. She looked at Lydia. "Is he making that up?"

"Probably not," said Lydia. She shrugged.

"Owen knows a million worthless facts nobody else cares about."

"It really was a man named Thomas Crapper," Owen said to Kate. "He was English."

"Okay," said Kate. "Go on."

"Millions of people in the United States flush their toilets every day," Owen said in what he hoped was a scholarly voice, "and yet none of them ever stops to wonder how a toilet actually works."

Kate laughed out loud. "You're too much, Owen."

"It's my parents' fault he talks like that," said Lydia. "They act like it's normal."

Owen lifted the top off the tank. He carefully put it down on the closed toilet lid. "Can everyone see?"

"You know, I don't think I've ever looked inside a toilet before," said Kate in an interested voice. She leaned forward to look, then immediately drew back. "Now I know why." She wrinkled her nose and made a face.

"Owen's been studying toilets since he was

about two," Lydia said. "We always used to know where he was by the sound of the toilet lid being scraped off the tank."

"Quiet, please," Owen said, frowning. He held his hand over the handle in a dramatic way. "I will now set the flushing action into operation."

He flushed.

Kate and Lydia moved in closer as the rod lifted, the hole was uncovered, the water rushed out, the white ball dropped, the stopper dropped back down to cover the hole, and the water started to rise. Owen described the process step by step.

When the noise finally stopped, there was a second of silence. Then Kate said, "That's kind of cool. You never think of it as being as simple as that."

She looked at the expression on Lydia's face. "Not that you ever think of it," she finished weakly.

"Can we go now?" said Lydia, her arms crossed over her chest.

"Certainly," Owen said. He stepped around in front of them and stood in the middle of the doorway. He held out his hand.

"That will be fifty cents, please."

"Fifty cents?" said Lydia. "You said it was free."

"The demonstration part was free," Owen said, "but someone has to pay for all the research that went into it."

He looked at Lydia's face. "Okay. . . . Two for fifty."

Kate laughed and reached into her pocket.

"Don't you dare!" shouted Lydia, grabbing Kate's arm and shoving Owen to one side. "Out of my way, weirdo."

"You're hilarious," Kate told Owen as Lydia dragged her out the door, forcing him up against the wall. She dropped a quarter into his out-stretched hand. "Thanks for the demo."

"At least *someone* appreciates the value of knowledge!" he shouted after Lydia. He put the top back on the tank. He looked at the money in his hand.

Twenty-five cents, he thought disgustedly. One lousy quarter for years of study.

A quarter was barely even money. *Dollars* were money. And Owen wanted them. Lots of them.

He had a wallet all ready for them.

Owen put the quarter in his pocket and headed for the stairs.

Ever since he had gotten that catalog, "Junk You Never Knew About," in the mail, Owen couldn't believe how many great things you could buy without even leaving the house. He had ten things on his list and it was still growing.

And then there was Joseph.

Owen went upstairs. Joseph had been his best friend since kindergarten. Last week, Joseph's mom had given his cat, Kitty, away. Owen had never seen Joseph so sad.

"She said she's not giving her *away*," Joseph had told him on the phone. "She said she's just sending Kitty to my grandmother until my dad outgrows his allergies."

"Can you outgrow allergies when you're as old as him?" Owen said.

"I don't think so." Joseph was quiet for a minute. "She said she's tired of cleaning up after Kitty's throw-up, too."

Even Owen couldn't argue with that. Kitty did throw up a lot.

"But *you* clean it up sometimes, don't you?" he said.

"Yeah, but there's usually a dry heap somewhere in the house."

"Why don't you take Kitty to the vet?" said Owen. "Maybe she has an incurable disease."

"It's not that," said Joseph. "She throws up hairballs."

"Hairballs?"

"It's what some cats do," Joseph said. "When

they clean themselves, they swallow the hair. Then they throw it up in a little ball with a bunch of other stuff."

"Oh." Owen searched for something positive to say. "Maybe she swallows it to protect your dad from his allergies," he said finally. "So he won't breathe it in. She was probably doing it for his own good."

"Yeah," said Joseph glumly, "and look where it got her."

There was nothing Owen could say that would cheer Joseph up. That was the worst part. Owen had always been able to cheer Joseph up before. Joseph always made him feel better, too.

That's what friends were for. Not being able to do that made Owen feel terrible.

Owen sat down at his desk and picked up the catalog. If the toilet demonstration wasn't going to turn out to be the moneymaker he had hoped, he'd have to think of something else.

He knew his mom wouldn't pay for a demonstration. He had tried to get her interested years ago.

All she said was that she'd seen the inside of a toilet tank more times than she cared to think.

Judging from the insides of the tanks of *our* toilets, he thought sourly, it certainly wasn't from cleaning them.

When he was in kindergarten, all he had wanted to be was a paleontologist. Now that he was in the third grade, all he wanted to be was rich.

The sooner, the better.

"I'm Not Ready Yet"

"Here's what I want for my birthday," said Owen. He came into the kitchen and put the catalog on the kitchen counter next to the sink.

"Right here." He opened it to a dog-eared page.

"You just had a birthday, Owen," said his mom. She leaned over to see where he was pointing and turned on the water to fill the bucket under the tap at the same time.

"Plastic vomit?" she said. "What would you do with it?"

"Lots of stuff," said Owen. "I could use it at parties and the cafeteria and everything." He frowned in concentration. "Either that or the dog poop. I can't decide."

"That's a tough one," said his mom.

"I'm not joking, Mom," Owen said. "I'm getting older. There are a lot of things I need."

"No one *needs* plastic vomit, Owen," said his mom.

She turned off the tap. "And I know you're getting older. If there are things you want, I suggest you try making some money. That's the best way I know to buy things."

"Well, then I need to get an allowance." Owen sat down at the kitchen table and wrapped his feet around the chair legs.

"Me, too," said Mrs. Foote. She poured some ammonia into the bucket. "How much do you think I should be paid to mop the kitchen floor every week?"

"I'm serious, Mom," Owen said. "Everyone I know gets an allowance."

"Fine," said Mrs. Foote. She put the bucket on the floor. "I'm willing to give it a try."

"It can't be like last year," Owen said. "Last year, you paid me two times and then you never paid me again."

"I think that's what usually happens. My sisters and I never got paid, either," said his mom. "Anyway, if I remember correctly, last year you told me you didn't think you were ready for an allowance yet."

"You gave me too much work," said Owen indignantly. "You wanted me to do all of *your* work."

"*My* work?" Mrs. Foote raised her right eyebrow. "Putting your dirty underwear in the laundry room is *my* work?"

"You always used to do it," Owen said.

"That's the point about getting an allowance, Owen," said his mom. "The older you get, the more capable you are of contributing to the household. Everyone in the family has to pitch in. Do you see a maid around here anywhere?"

"Okay, okay, don't start getting all complicated," Owen said. "This is why I hate talking about stuff with you. You always give me a big lecture. I don't want to talk about responsibility. I want to talk about money."

Mrs. Foote laughed. "You put your finger right

on it. Parents see allowance as responsibility, and children see it as money."

"Right." His mom was finally getting the point. "And since kids are the ones getting it," Owen said, "we should know. So how much will you give me?"

"You mean, what do you have to do?"

Owen sighed. "Okay. What do I have to do? But don't go crazy."

"Okay." His mom leaned against the counter. "Let's see. You have to make your bed and clean your room, unload the dishwasher, put your dirty clothes in the laundry, and feed Major," she said. "All without my having to remind you."

"All that?" said Owen. "For how much?"

"How about . . ." Mrs. Foote looked up as if she were consulting a list written on the ceiling. ". . . three dollars."

"How often?"

"How often?" said his mom, raising both eyebrows. "Once a week."

"Once a week?" Owen jumped up out of his

chair. "You want me to do all that for three dollars once a week? You're joking."

"I think three dollars sounds about right for an eight-year-old, Owen."

"That's only twelve dollars a month," said Owen. He grabbed a pencil and scribbled on the back of an envelope. "One hundred and—"

He looked at his mother with his mouth hanging open. "That's only one hundred and twenty dollars a year!" he said. "You want to skin out of all your jobs, and make me run the whole house, for less than two hundred dollars a year? That's practically slave labor."

His mom gave a shout of laughter. "You amaze me, Owen," she said, "you really do."

"I'm serious, Mom. You could be arrested," Owen said. "If I reported you, you'd get into real trouble with child labor laws. Three dollars?"

"Actually, Einstein, it's one hundred and fifty-six dollars a year." Lydia grabbed an apple from a bowl on the kitchen counter as she came into the room.

"How come Owen's getting three dollars?"

she said, biting into it. "I only got two-fifty when I was his age."

Tiny pieces of apple sprayed out of her mouth.

"Lydia, please . . ." said Mrs. Foote.

"Okay, one hundred and fifty-six," said Owen, scribbling again, "but now you get fifteen."

"Wait a minute, Owen," said Mrs. Foote. "Lydia vacuums the entire house, cleans her room and changes her bed, dusts the living room, and cleans all three bathrooms."

"Yeah," said Lydia, "and does her own laundry." She stuck out her tongue.

"I'll tell you what." Mrs. Foote looked Owen straight in the eye. "You clean your own bathroom and I'll make it four dollars."

"Are you joking?" said Owen. He thought about the dried yellow stains on the floor around the toilet and the little heaps of hardened toothpaste all over the sink.

"My bathroom's disgusting," he said. "Forget it, Mom. I'm not ready for an allowance yet."

"That's what you said last year," said Lydia.

"Mind your own business."

"Owen likes to make money by not doing anything," said Lydia. "Remember the time he tried to sell the rocks from the driveway?"

"They had faces painted on them," Owen said.

"Yeah, right. You made little scribbles with a marker."

"I was about four years old, okay?"

"And what about the Dinosaur Information Booth you made in first grade?" Lydia said. "The one where you wore your Triceratops costume from Halloween. That was a big idea."

"I thought he looked sweet," said Mrs. Foote. "I loved that costume."

"That's all you know," Owen said to Lydia. "That was a great idea. Mr. White gave me two dollars."

"That's because he was sorry for you for being such a *loser*."

"Lydia, please," said Mrs. Foote again. "Stay out of this."

She stuck the mop in the bucket. "You still

have to clean your room, Owen. You can get paid for it or not. It's up to you. But I think you're going to find that if you want to have money, you have to be willing to work for it."

"I don't want to work for it," Owen muttered. "I want to earn it."

"Earn, work, what's the difference?" said Lydia.

"If you don't know, I suggest you look them up," said Owen in the annoying way their mother did when they didn't know a word. "I'll let you know when I'm ready, Mom."

He grabbed an apple and skinned out of the room before Lydia could say anything. He knew he should quit while he was ahead.

Well, not ahead. He couldn't believe he had gotten his math wrong. But at least equal.

With his mom, forget it. Owen went into the study and flopped down on the couch. When it came to money, his mom was ridiculous. All she thought about was work.

Owen liked the sound of *earn* better. He didn't know how to explain it, but *earn* sounded like more fun.

Easier, kind of.

You could earn money while you were wearing a suit and a tie. When you worked for it, you had to lift heavy things and get all sweaty.

He looked out the window and saw his dad pushing the wheelbarrow across the yard.

That was it! Owen sat up.

He should have talked to his dad.

Men understood things like money better than girls.

Owen went over to the desk to look for a piece of paper and pencil.

Just wait.

Someday he'd be a millionaire. He'd live in a mansion with maids and drive expensive cars. He'd be able to buy anything he wanted.

He might let his mom come over to cook for him.

But not Lydia. She could get down on her knees and beg him to let her swim in his pool. He'd say no.

The only way he'd let her come is if she offered to clean the bathrooms.

Yeeeaaahhh. Owen grinned. He liked that idea a lot. He'd definitely let Lydia in to clean the bathrooms.

But the minute she was done, she'd have to leave.

He might even pay her.

But not a penny more than three dollars a week.

3

THE TWO-THOUSAND-LEAF PILE

"Hi, Dad. Need any help?"

"Are you actually offering?" said Mr. Foote.

"Kind of." Owen fell into step beside his dad as he pushed the empty wheelbarrow back across the yard. "I was thinking. You know that pile of leaves next to the garage?"

"The one I asked you and Lydia to pick up last week?"

"Yeah. How about if I rake it up—and bag it," Owen said with emphasis, so his dad would realize what a great deal he was getting, "for one cent a leaf."

"One cent a leaf?" said Mr. Foote.

"Not bad, huh?" Owen pulled a piece of paper out of his pocket. "I estimated there are about two thousand leaves in that pile, give or take a few."

He consulted his calculations. "At that low rate, it will only cost you twenty dollars for the whole job."

"Twenty dollars for one pile of leaves?" said Mr. Foote. "Is that a bargain?"

"It's a big pile," said Owen.

"I know it is, Owen. I raked it," said his dad. "And I was kind of hoping you would pick it up, gratis."

"Gratis?" said Owen suspiciously. "What does that mean?"

"Free of charge," said his dad. "As a member of the family, and all that."

Owen made a disgusted face. "You know, you and Mom are getting a little too carried away with this 'member of the family' business all of a sudden." He turned to leave. "Forget it."

"Where are you going?" said his dad.

"Joseph called yesterday. He wants me to come over to see the turtle his dad found in their basement," said Owen. "Mom said I could."

"Okay," said Mr. Foote, "but hurry back. The two-thousand-leaf pile will be waiting."

———

"Wait till you see him," Joseph said. "He's the cutest thing."

Owen followed Joseph up the stairs and into his bedroom. Joseph led him over to his book-case. There was a glass bowl filled with water sitting on it.

"Look. He's a box turtle," said Joseph.

Owen looked. A dirty green turtle no bigger than a quarter was swimming around and around. His tiny feet were paddling back and forth as if he were trying to get a grip on a slippery surface.

"You have to put a rock in there," Owen said, "so he has something to rest on."

"Why? Do you think he's drowning?" Joseph said anxiously.

"I don't think turtles can drown," Owen said. "But they like to take it easy every once in a while."

The turtle was heading straight toward the glass. He bounced off the side of the bowl and bobbed around a little as if he were stunned. Then he started off in another direction.

"He's going to knock himself out," said Owen.

"Do you think the bowl is too small?"

"Joseph." Owen put his hand on Joseph's arm. "Take it easy. I was joking. He's fine."

"Yeah. Isn't he great?" Joseph picked up a spoon and jabbed lightly at the turtle's nose. "I'm training him to defend himself."

The turtle blinked and pulled in his head.

"You don't have to do that," Owen said. "He knows how to bite better than you do. He's a snapping turtle."

"He is?" Joseph yanked the spoon back from in front of the turtle's nose. "Are you sure?"

"Look at his shell," said Owen. "A box turtle has a high-domed shell, and a snapping turtle has a flat one."

He put his head down so that he and the turtle were practically nose-to-nose. "Yep, he's a snapper, all right."

"My dad thought it was a box turtle," said Joseph in a worried voice. "I don't think my mom will like having a dangerous animal in the house."

Owen wanted to say, "Your mom doesn't like having *any* animal in the house," but he didn't. Joseph was so happy to have a pet. Any pet.

"Don't worry, she'll never know the difference," he said instead. "Besides, it's not like it's a man-eating tiger, or anything."

"But what if it bites me and draws blood?" said Joseph. "What about salmonella?"

"You'll have to let it go long before it's big enough to hurt you," said Owen. "Wild animals don't do well in captivity. Remember my salamanders?"

Last summer, Owen had found two salamanders in the stream that ran through the woods behind his house. He built a home for them in an aquarium with a small pond, a sandy beach, and a log they could climb on.

He put in soft moss and spritzed the sides with a water bottle. It was called an "environment," he told Joseph. He was planning on taking it to show his teacher when school started.

Within a week, one salamander was dead and the other one didn't look happy.

"You mean, he's going to die?" said Joseph. He looked from Owen to the turtle, then back at Owen again. "Here? In my room?"

"Joseph, calm down," said Owen. "He has to die somewhere."

"But what if I wake up one morning and he's not breathing," said Joseph. "What do I do?"

"You let him go way before that," said Owen patiently. "The rule in our house now is four days."

"But I just got him," said Joseph. "We haven't even started to bond." He slumped down onto the floor. "Now I'm depressed. First Kitty, now this."

Joseph's mom was a family therapist. She talked about things like bonding and nurturing all the time. She had Joseph convinced that bonding was right up there with eating.

That's why Owen couldn't figure out why she'd given Kitty away. She should have had Mr. Hobbs wear one of those masks over his mouth instead. He could take it off when he went to work.

If she'd done that, Joseph wouldn't have to be bonding with a turtle that was first going to bite him, then die.

Owen sat down on the floor next to him. "What you need to do is buy an animal that's been bred in captivity, Joseph. You can keep those things forever."

"Great idea," said Joseph glumly. "Trouble is, the only money I have is the check my grandmother gave me for my birthday. My parents said I have to put it into the bank for college."

"I know what you mean," said Owen. "My

parents won't give me any money unless I work for it."

They sat there in glum silence for a while. Then Owen hit his knee with his fist. "We have to think of a way to make some money," he said. "There's no other solution."

"We could sell lemonade," said Joseph hopefully. "Like we did in kindergarten."

"No, we're too old," Owen said. "People like to buy lemonade from cute little kids who write the letters on their signs backwards."

"Yeah, I guess," said Joseph. "Anyway, my mom said that if I want to sell anything that has ingredients again, I have to pay her back for buying them."

"No fair," said Owen. "That would cut into our profits." He scowled. "I hope she doesn't tell my mom about that."

"I bet your mom already knows," said Joseph.

"Boy, they sure are getting mean," Owen said. He stood up. "Come on. Let's get some paper and make a list. There are a ton of ideas that don't take ingredients."

"Like what?"

"I don't know. We have to think of them."

"Right." Joseph got up and went over to his desk.

"You write down the ideas, and I'll write down the animals we want to buy," Owen said. He grabbed two books for them to write on and jumped onto Joseph's bed. "We'll make so much money, we'll probably have to open a bank account."

"Yeah, a savings account *and* a checking account," said Joseph, plunking down next to him. "But right now, I guess we should pay for everything in cash."

"Yeah," said Owen. He liked the way that sounded.

In cash.

It sounded a lot better than out of cash, any day.

4

FISHING FOR PROFIT

"Mom? Where are you?"

"Up here," Owen heard his mom yell. "In the bedroom."

Owen took the stairs two at a time. "You won't believe the great idea Joseph and I have," he said, crashing into his parents' room.

He slumped against the bed, breathing hard. "We're going to be rich."

"Another lemonade stand, I suppose," said Lydia. She leaned against her mother's door with her arms full of clean clothing. "That's original."

"I'm not talking to you," said Owen, "so butt out."

"Owen, I've asked you not to use that expression," said Mrs. Foote. "Lydia, this doesn't concern you. Please close the door and finish what you were doing."

"Okay," Lydia drawled, "but don't say I didn't warn you when Owen hits you up for financing."

She took a neat step back into the hall a second before Owen slammed the door in her face.

"Owen, please," sighed Mrs. Foote. "I don't know who's worse, you or Lydia."

"That's easy," Owen said. "Lydia."

He stood in front of his mother and clasped his hands together in front of his chest. "I need to ask you for one thing."

"Financing?" said Mrs. Foote.

"No. Can Joseph and I borrow our video camera?"

"What for?" said his mom.

"I can't tell you yet," Owen said. "We have to practice first. But can we?"

"I guess so," said Mrs. Foote, "but Dad or I will have to supervise. What are you filming?"

"Thanks, Mom, you're the greatest," said

Owen. He yanked the door open. "I'll tell you later!"

He sprinted back down the stairs, through the kitchen, and out into the garage. He grabbed his fishing pole and his tackle box.

Then he peered around the corner of the house.

The coast was clear. His dad was probably inside, doing the crossword puzzle.

Owen ran across his yard into the Baileys' yard next door. They had a pond out in the back where they let Owen fish as long as he threw back anything he caught.

And today Owen wasn't fishing for fish. He was fishing for profit.

He and Joseph had a plan that was going to make them rich. They were going to make a kids' fishing video.

It was Owen's idea. He knew all about fishing videos. He and his dad had been watching them on television for years. Owen loved them.

They showed a few guys sitting around in boats, fishing. The guys talked about the perfect bait, how smart fish were, how to set your hook—important things like that.

Owen had learned a lot watching those videos. But he had never seen one with kids in it. Only grownups. He thought kids would much rather watch their own video. And he and Joseph were going to film it.

They were going to call it "Kids Fishing." Owen bet they would sell a million copies.

He was going to be the star because Joseph's face broke out in spots when he had to talk in front of people.

Owen didn't want it to look as if fishing made kids allergic.

Joseph was already at the pond. Owen ran over and put his tackle box on the ground. "My mom said we could," he said. "I told her we have to practice first."

"Great," Joseph said. "How should we start?"

"How about if I make some things up and if we like the way they sound, we'll write them down."

"Good idea."

Owen took a lure out of his box and clipped it on his line.

Joseph held an imaginary camera up in front of his face. "Ready?"

"Ready."

"All right," said Joseph. "Lights, camera, action!"

Owen pushed his shoulders back and cleared his throat. "Today, what we're using is your basic bass lure," he said in his best announcer's voice. "I'm going to set this baby on the water and see what's biting out there."

The men in the videos on television always called their lures "baby," Owen had noticed. When he thought about it, so did the guys who drove race cars. They said things like "Let's open this baby up and see what she'll do" and "Look at that baby go."

Owen wasn't sure if it was because they felt protective about things like lures and cars, or because they felt the lure or the car was in their power. So they were the boss.

Either way, Owen liked the way it sounded.

He and Joseph watched his lure fly out over the pond and plunk down in the water. Owen gave it time to settle to the bottom, then jerked on the line and started to reel it back in.

He looked to the side, as if he were talking to the camera. "Later, I'll talk about your basic bobber, but right now I want to show you a few techniques."

"Sounds good so far," Joseph said in a low voice.

Owen reeled the lure in and started to whip his pole back and forth over his head like a fly fisherman. That's what the fishermen on TV did when they were trying to position their lures to hit the perfect spot.

It was amazing. They could flip their poles back and forth in the air a few times, then put their lure down exactly where they wanted it.

There always seemed to be a huge fish waiting to take it, too.

Owen flicked his line back over his head one last time, then cast forward.

Nothing happened.

He flicked the line again and felt a slight tug on his left ear. "Where is it?" He craned his head around to look back over his shoulder. "Is it caught on a bush or something?"

"No," said Joseph. "You caught your ear."

Owen stopped tugging. "My ear?"

Joseph came over and stood next to him. "Yeah. You kind of caught it on the rim. Don't keep pulling on it."

Owen kept his eyes straight ahead as he bent his knees to rest the end of his pole on the ground. All he could feel was a slight stinging, like a mosquito bite.

"Is it bleeding?"

"Not really," said Joseph. "I don't think there's much blood in your ear. It's mostly cartilage."

Owen stared straight ahead and blinked. "What should we do?"

"I think I can pull it back out," Joseph said. He peered at Owen's ear. "It's not a very big hook."

"No, don't." Owen's voice rose up. "It's got barbs on the end. You'll tear my ear off."

He cupped his hand over his ear. He couldn't see the hook, but he could imagine it. That was worse.

"This will work, Owen," Joseph said. He was on his knees, rummaging around in the tackle box. "I know it will."

He stood up and held out a pair of needle-nosed pliers. He and Owen used them to pull the hook out of a fish when the fish had swallowed it. "I can cut the hook with these things and slide it right out."

"No." Owen pressed his hand tighter over his ear. He could feel the metal of the hook against his palm. "I think I should go home."

"I can do it, Owen," said Joseph. "It won't hurt. I promise."

He sounded very calm. He looked calm, too. Somehow, Owen knew he could trust him. He squeezed his eyes shut and took his hand away from his ear. "Okay. But hurry."

Owen took a deep breath and held it. He felt Joseph's fingers on his ear.

Then he heard a snap.

"It's out."

Owen opened his eyes. Joseph was holding the hook up in front of his face. "All done."

He sounded exactly like the nurse did when she held up the needle to show Owen that a shot was over. Owen felt the same powerful surge of relief.

Joseph pulled a handkerchief out of his pocket and handed it to him. "Hold this on it."

Owen pressed the handkerchief over his ear, then held it away to inspect it. There was a tiny speck of blood on it. It was so small, it was hard to see.

But it was big enough for Owen.

"You can't even tell there was anything there," Joseph said, looking at Owen's ear. "It's amazing."

Owen put the handkerchief back over his ear and sagged down onto the grass. He looked at the handkerchief again.

Another tiny speck.

"I thought you hated the sight of blood," he said.

"There wasn't any until I took the hook out," Joseph said. He shrugged. "It was kind of interesting."

He put the pliers back into Owen's tackle box and shut it. "We'd better go tell your mom, just in case. You might have to get a tetanus shot."

"She'll probably faint just thinking about it," said Owen. He got up and followed Joseph across the Baileys' yard. "When I smashed my finger with the hammer one time, she wanted to put the hammer away until I was older. Good thing my dad stopped her. She probably would have made me wait till I was eighteen before I hammered another nail. This is going to make her a nervous wreck about the fishing video."

"Maybe we should try the second idea on our list instead," said Joseph.

"You think so?"

"Yeah. We don't have to practice, and it's not as dangerous."

"I guess you're right," said Owen. He was glad Joseph had said it and not him. Now that he thought about it, it might be a good idea to practice with a sinker for a while, instead of a hook. It would be pretty embarrassing, doing such a dumb thing in front of a camera.

"If it was me, I would have fainted," Joseph was saying. "But you didn't do anything. You just stood there."

"I couldn't really feel it," said Owen. "And not being able to see it helped. It's like it was no big deal."

It was true. Now that it was over, it didn't seem scary at all. It actually felt kind of cool.

It wasn't as if he had cried or anything. As a matter of fact, Owen realized, he hadn't even thought about crying.

Not once.

He took the handkerchief away from his ear.

No new blood.

"I don't need this dumb thing anymore," he said, scornfully. He handed it to Joseph.

"You can keep it as a souvenir if you want," said Joseph.

"No, thanks. There's not enough blood," Owen said. "I want Lydia to think there was blood gushing all over the place. She'll freak out."

"Okay." Joseph looked down at his red T-shirt. "I'll tell her my shirt used to be white."

"Cool," said Owen. All of a sudden, he felt great. Like a real veteran. A member of the brotherhood of fishermen.

He bet all those guys on TV had hooked themselves sometime or other. "That reminds me of the time I got a nasty bass hook in my thumb," they'd say. "That was one big hook."

Or their leg. Or their back.

Maybe even their ear.

The more Owen thought about it, the better he felt.

It was amazing how getting a hook in your ear could make you feel so good.

5

No Snakes, No Skunks

"Thanks for coming over, Owen."

Mrs. Cook held a tissue over her nose and sneezed. "Kirby is dying to go out, and I feel terrible."

"You don't look so good," Owen said.

Mrs. Cook's nostrils were rimmed with red. Her upper lip looked as if she'd been working on it with sandpaper.

"Joseph and I are starting a pet-walking service," Owen said. "This will be good practice."

Kirby was rushing around, yapping excitedly. He was the Cooks' Jack Russell terrier. He could bounce straight up in the air with all four feet off the ground at the same time.

That was what he was doing now. He made Owen think of a wind-up toy at high speed.

"He's pretty frisky for an old dog," said Owen.

"He's excited to see you," said Mrs. Cook. "Aren't you, Kirby?" She leaned down to clip the leash to Kirby's collar.

"He's quite a bouncer."

Mrs. Cook gave a little laugh. "I know. He chipped my sister's front tooth a few weeks ago when she bent down to pet him. Kirby jumped straight up and smacked her in the mouth. Didn't you, Kirby?"

She patted Kirby's head as if chipping someone's tooth was something he should be proud of. She sure doesn't sound very sorry about it, Owen thought. He'd have to make a note for their records.

Anyone who got the job of walking Kirby had to make sure they stood up straight.

While Mrs. Cook told him which route Kirby

liked best, Kirby started sniffing around Owen's ankles.

"I think he's getting used to me," Owen said.

He looked down just as Kirby was lifting his leg against Owen's pants.

So did Mrs. Cook.

"Kirby!" she shrieked.

But Kirby was way ahead of her.

"So that's 'No old dogs,' either," Owen said, scribbling. He rubbed his leg, in his clean sweatpants, against the rug as if he'd never get it dry enough.

"What did Mrs. Cook do?" said Joseph.

"She wanted to wipe it off, but I got the heck out of there," said Owen. "She called my mom to apologize. She said it was because Kirby is old and has a hard time holding it."

"Gross," said Joseph.

Owen leaned his elbows on the large sheet of paper on the floor in front of them. "Maybe 'Young dogs preferred' sounds better."

"Yeah. The list of animals we don't want to walk is getting pretty long," said Joseph.

Owen sat back on his heels and held the sign out as if it were a painting and they were artists analyzing it.

"Pet-Walking Service," he read. "Low Rates. Experienced Walkers."

He looked at Joseph. "Do you think it sounds like we know how to walk pets, or just plain old walk?"

Joseph chewed on the inside of his mouth while he thought. "Just plain old walk," he said finally. "I'm not sure it even sounds as if we like pets very much."

They looked glumly at the sign.

"No snakes, no large dogs, no mean dogs, no strong dogs, no skunks," Joseph read, "and now no old dogs."

"We have to protect ourselves somehow, don't we?" said Owen. "Anyway, you're the one who wanted to add skunks. I don't know any-one who even owns a skunk."

Joseph shook his head. "I tell you, Owen,

when my uncle thought he had de-skunked their pet skunk, Seymour, and put him in the car to take him to Maine with us, it was terrible."

He pinched his nose shut. "Ten whole hours."

Owen threw the marker down on the sign. "This'll never work," he said in a disgusted voice.

He crossed his arms over his chest. "What if everyone waits until the last minute to hire us? What if, to save money, they decide to have their dog walked once a week, so by the time we get there, it's like a ticking pee-bomb that can't even make it out of the house?"

"If I get it on my pants, my mom will make me quit," said Joseph.

"We'll never be able to buy this stuff," Owen said. He reached up and grabbed the catalog off his bed. "Look at it. It's awesome."

He jabbed a page with his finger. Joseph crawled closer and leaned over Owen's shoulder.

"A cushion you hide under the seat so when someone sits down, they make a rude noise," Owen said.

"My cousin had one of those," Joseph said. "They're great. They sound so real."

"And look at these." Owen flipped to another dog-eared page. "Tricks, for only ninety-nine cents. Look at those fake bullet holes."

"Plastic vomit," said Joseph, reading. "Cool."

"Cool, all right," said Owen.

Suddenly, he had an idea. "Hey!" he said, sitting up. "We could leave the vomit around your house so your mom will think it's still happening, and take Kitty back."

Joseph frowned. "Who will she think's doing it?"

"Oh . . . I hadn't thought of that." Owen sank

back against the bed. "We can't buy any of this stuff anyway."

He closed the catalog and threw it back on his bed. "Not at the rate we're going."

"Joseph," they heard Owen's mom call, "your mother's here!"

"Great, and now you've got to leave," said Owen.

"I have a violin lesson," Joseph said meekly. "Sorry."

"It's okay." Owen stood up and followed him down the stairs. His mother was standing at the bottom.

"Bye, Mrs. Foote," said Joseph.

"Bye, Joseph. Why so glum?" she said to Owen. "Aren't you two due over at Anthony's?"

"I'm going over after my lesson," said Joseph.

"Anthony just wants us to come over so he can brag about his new computer," said Owen. "He's always bragging about his stuff. His parents buy him anything he wants."

"He even has his own balcony," said Joseph.

Owen's mom was smiling as she held open the front door.

"And don't start giving me any lectures about how guilty they feel because they work all the time," Owen said to her. "I'm not in the mood."

"Okay, I won't," said his mom. "But it's true."

She reached out to ruffle his hair, but Owen ducked out of her reach.

"Be home in time for dinner," she called after him.

Joseph's mother was waiting in the car. "Hi, Mrs. Hobbs," Owen said. "Bye, Joseph."

"See you later, Owen."

Owen jammed his hands in his pockets and hunched his shoulders. Anthony had his own television, his own VCR, and his own CD player.

Owen scuffed his feet along the road, trying to make a dust cloud.

Now he had his own computer. He could stay in his room for the rest of his life and never have to come out.

Never have to share the television he was

only allowed to watch on weekends with his bratty sister like Owen did.

It wasn't fair.

The dust cloud was almost up to his knees. He could barely see his feet.

Good, he thought bitterly. He scuffed his feet even more.

He hoped he ruined his shoes.

It would serve his mom right.

6

"WHAT DO YOU KNOW ABOUT PONDS?"

Owen didn't hear the car pull up next to him until a familiar voice said, "Hi, Owen."

Owen looked up. "Oh, hi, Mr. White."

"You're just the man I was hoping to see." Mr. White leaned his arms on the steering wheel and smiled.

"What about?" said Owen.

He liked Mr. White. Even though Mr. White was almost old enough to be Owen's grandfather, he and Owen were friends.

If Owen walked by the Whites' house at the end of the street when Mr. White was outside, he always stopped to talk. Mr. White said he liked to hear what Owen had to say.

Sometimes they talked about animals, sometimes they talked about things that had happened at school. Mr. White didn't treat Owen as if he was only a kid. He acted as if Owen was someone with opinions Mr. White wanted to hear.

Like now.

"What do you know about ponds?" he said.

"Ponds?" Owen had to think for a minute. "Well, my dad and I have been talking about building one in our back yard. We must have drawn a million plans by now. And I have a book that tells you how to build them. It's really about survival, but they have a section about ponds, for some reason. I like ponds."

"I kind of thought you might," said Mr. White. "The reason I ask is that I'm about to start digging one in my back yard, and I thought maybe you'd be willing to come act as my consultant."

"Sure," said Owen.

"I bet you know a thing or two about goldfish, too," said Mr. White. "You seem to know a lot more about animals than I do."

"I know they're from China," said Owen, "and that they're not always gold. Some of them are kind of whitish orange. Scoobie's Pet World has some beautiful ones. I go in there all the time."

"My wife wants the gold ones," said Mr. White. "She's been after me for years to build her a goldfish pond. I'm going to surprise her for our thirty-fifth wedding anniversary."

"You might want to look at Japanese koi," said Owen, warming to the subject. "They've got patterns on the top that look great when you look down on them. Like you do when they're in a pond. But they're more expensive."

"Scoobie's Pet World is the place, huh?" said Mr. White. "I'll have to have a look."

"You have to make sure you dig the pond deep enough if you're going to put in goldfish," Owen said, "or the raccoons will get them. There are a lot of raccoons around."

"Oh, I know. We used to have a family of them we fed by hand on the back porch," Mr. White said. "But thanks for the reminder. I hadn't thought of that."

"I saw a picture of two of them in a nature magazine one time," said Owen. "They were scooping fish out of a pond like they were at a buffet dinner."

Mr. White laughed. "I knew you were the right man for the job. Listen: Our anniversary is next weekend, and Mrs. White is off visiting our daughter until then. So it's now or never. I start tomorrow. Are you with me?"

He made it sound exciting. Like he was asking Owen to join him on a dangerous military mission or something.

"I'm with you," said Owen. "What time?"

"Come as early as you want," said Mr. White. "I'll be out there soon as the sun comes up."

"Okay," Owen said. "See you tomorrow."

He waved as Mr. White pulled away. When the car turned the corner, he jumped up and punched his fist in the air.

Yes!

A consultant. Owen liked the sound of that. A consultant was someone who knew something.

That was him, all right. He knew plenty of stuff.

Owen gave a little hop. He was suddenly full of energy. His body felt like a bottle of soda when you first open the top. It was filled with bubbles, all rushing to the top.

He could hardly stand still.

He had to get over to Anthony's fast, so that he could get back home again and check on his facts. Wait till Mr. White saw his book with the stuff about ponds!

Owen walked along, bouncing up onto the tips of his toes. And wait until he told Anthony about his consulting job! Even parents couldn't buy you a consulting job. You had to know something all on your own to get one.

But now that he thought about it, he didn't feel like bragging to Anthony.

That's how good he felt.

Maybe bragging was something you did when you didn't feel too sure about something, Owen thought.

Then he stopped thinking and ran.

SWEATING LIKE A PIG

"What do you think?"

Mr. White leaned on the end of his shovel and wiped his forehead with the back of his arm. "Think Mrs. White will like it?"

"I think she'll love it," Owen said. He stepped over the hose that was filling the pond with water and sat down on the chair Mr. White had brought out for him. "It's great."

"It sure took us long enough," said Mr. White. He looked at his watch. "It's almost one o'clock."

"It didn't seem like that long," said Owen. "It was fun."

"It was, wasn't it?" Mr. White bent down and picked up the spade and the shovel. "I'm going to put these back in the garage and get myself something cold to drink, Owen. Can I get you another soda?"

"No, thanks." Owen picked up the half-empty can on the ground by his side. "I still have some."

"I'll be right back," said Mr. White. "When you think the water is deep enough, turn it off, would you?"

"Sure."

Owen took a swig of his soda. It was the second one he'd had today. Mr. White had given him the first one at nine o'clock.

Owen hadn't had a soda at nine o'clock in the morning in his whole life. His mom didn't really like him and Lydia to drink soda at all.

She said she didn't believe in it.

"Soda's not something you *believe* in, Mom," Lydia had said. "We're not talking about Santa Claus here. We're talking about a drink."

"How can you not believe in it?" Owen had added. "It's right there in the can."

Even then, their mom might not have changed her mind. Luckily, Mr. Foote had taken their side.

"I think that, as a grown man and father of two, I have the right to drink what I want in my own house," he had said with dignity. "And as much as you may hate to hear this, dear, I like soda, too."

Mrs. Foote had had to give in. But she only let them drink it on holidays and weekends. Then she made such a big deal about them brushing their teeth every time, it almost wasn't worth it.

But no matter how many sodas she had let Owen have, none of them had ever tasted as good as the warm, flat one he was drinking now.

He leaned back in his chair and watched the water inching up the side of the liner.

Not bad for his first consulting job. Not bad at all.

First, he had showed Mr. White the section on ponds in his book. They studied all the diagrams. Mr. White said he liked the oval ones, but that Mrs. White wanted a round one. So that's the shape they picked.

It had to be four feet wide, Mr. White said, because that's all the space they had. So he tied a two-foot piece of string to a stick and stuck the stick in the ground. Then Owen walked around in a circle, holding the string out taut, while Mr. White walked behind him and cut the outline with a spade.

Then they started to dig. They took turns. It wasn't too hard once they had dug through the grass. But it was hot. Owen could feel the sweat trickling down his back as he shoveled.

"I think I'll take this off," he said, pulling off his T-shirt. He threw it to the ground and looked down at his chest.

Bare-chested, it was called. He was working bare-chested.

Owen hoped the sweat would make little tracks through the dirt on his back. He had seen photographs of men without their shirts on working in fields and hot places like that. Their backs always looked sweaty and dirty.

They looked hot, all right, but they also looked strong.

When it was time to dig the deeper, fish-hiding section in the middle, Mr. White said Owen should be the one to decide how deep to make it.

"Go ahead," he said, leaning on his shovel. "You're the engineer."

Owen walked around the pond a few times, thinking.

"I think we should dig a little section about a foot deep and a foot wide," he said finally. "It will be like a secret hiding place. When a raccoon comes, bam!" He hit his fist against his palm. "Those fish will run for it."

"Or swim for it, in this case," said Mr. White.

"Right," said Owen.

Finally, they were done. They lined the whole pond with a black liner and put flat stones all around the edge.

Now was the best part of all, Owen thought. Sitting and admiring their work with the sun on his back and the smell of dirt in the air.

Mr. White came back and sat down beside him. For a while, they just sat and watched the pond filling up. They didn't even have to talk.

"It's amazing," Owen said at one point. "This used to be a yard without a pond. Now it's a yard *with* a pond."

"I know exactly what you mean," said Mr. White.

They sat some more. Then Mr. White slapped his hands on his knees and stood up. "What do you say? Want to come with me to Scoobie's and help me buy those Japanese koi?"

"Sure," Owen said. He stood up, too. "I can show you the spotted newts they have. They're like the salamanders I found last year, the ones I told you about that died. The ones at Scoobie's are bred in captivity, so they live longer."

"I'll tell you what," said Mr. White. He reached into his back pocket. "I'll go in and take a shower while you run home and make sure it's okay with your mother.

"And here." Mr. White held something out in front of him. "Maybe she'll let you buy one of those newts you have your eye on."

Owen looked at it. It was a twenty-dollar bill.

"For me?" he said.

"For a job well done," said Mr. White. He gave the money a little shake. "Go on, take it."

Owen took it. It was a brand-new twenty-dollar bill. It was so stiff, it looked fake. Owen couldn't believe it was his.

"I didn't know you were going to pay me," he said in an awed voice.

"I hired you, didn't I?"

"I didn't think you were really *hiring* me," said Owen. "I thought you just wanted some free advice, like you always do."

"Free advice!" Mr. White threw back his head and laughed for a long time. Then he looked at Owen and clamped his hand on Owen's shoulder. "This doesn't mean you're going to start back-charging me, does it?"

Owen felt his face get hot.

"No, I—"

"I'm only kidding," said Mr. White. He gave Owen's shoulder a little shake. "You're a good boy, Owen. Take the money. You earned it."

"Okay," said Owen. "Thanks a lot."

"Thank *you*," said Mr. White. "I couldn't have done it without you." He put the leftover pieces of liner and the string into his wheelbarrow. "Think you can be ready in half an hour?"

"Sure," said Owen, still looking at the money in his hand. "See you then."

He walked across the yard in a daze. The minute his feet hit the pavement, he started to run.

He couldn't believe it. Twenty dollars. Twenty whole dollars, and they were all his. Wait till he showed his mom!

His mom. Owen stopped dead in his tracks.

He knew his mom. She had a million rules. Rules about how to act and how to treat people. About what to do and what not to do. Owen knew she'd worry that Mr. White was being too generous. She'd think he was just being nice.

Owen looked at the money in his hand with

the first seeds of doubt in his mind. A minute ago, it had been the most exciting thing he'd ever had.

Now he wasn't even sure he'd be allowed to keep it.

"Twenty dollars?" Mrs. Foote's eyebrows shot up under her bangs. "My goodness."

"Let me see that," said Lydia. She snatched the bill out of Owen's hand.

"Give it back!" Owen yelled, grabbing it back. "You'll wrinkle it."

"Lydia, leave it alone," said Mrs. Foote. Then, in a worried voice, "I don't know, Owen. That's a lot of money."

"I worked hard for it," Owen said. He smoothed the bill carefully on the counter. "You wouldn't believe how hot it was."

"I'm sure it was," said his mom. "But I think maybe Mr. White was being overly generous."

"He's always been that way with Owen," said Lydia. "I don't get it."

"You're no fair, Mom," Owen said. "First, you tell me I have to be willing to work for my money, then you tell me I've been paid too much."

He suddenly knew that what he was saying was right.

"I'm keeping it," he said firmly. "I worked hard for this money. If you don't believe me, look at my back."

He turned around so they could see his back. Please be sweaty and dirty, he pleaded silently. Please.

"Euw, get away from me." Lydia held her nose and stepped back. "You're disgusting."

Owen felt a surge of manly pride. "I told you so."

"But twenty dollars, Owen," said his mom. "You're only eight."

"What does age have to do with it?" said Lydia, still holding her nose. "He's sweating like a pig."

"Yeah," said Owen. He liked that description. "You should smell my underarms."

He lifted up his arm in Lydia's direction. She screamed and ran out of the room.

"All right, Owen, that's enough," said his mom. She tried not to smile, but Owen could tell she thought it was funny. "Your 'underarms'?" she said. She shook her head. "Whatever happened to my innocent little boy?"

"He became a man!" Owen shouted. He stood sideways and made a muscle-man pose. "Look at those pecs."

Mrs. Foote laughed. "I guess you're right," she said finally. "But you make sure you thank Mr. White. And go put on some clean clothes."

"I will!" said Owen. He ran to the door, then stopped and turned around. "One more thing."

"What?" said his mom.

"Can I buy a newt? Please?"

"Oh, Owen."

"Please, Mom?" Owen came back into the room. "You won't have to do a thing, I promise. I'll take care of it. I'll clean the aquarium and feed it and everything."

He screwed up his face into its most pleading look. "Please?"

Mrs. Foote closed her eyes, then opened them. "What does it eat?"

Yes! Owen knew it was all right. As long as it wasn't going to be like a snake, cornering a terrified mouse once a day up in his room, his mom would say it was okay.

"Nothing alive," he said quickly. "Synthetic newt food. I'll pay for it."

"Okay," said Mrs. Foote. "But I don't want to have to lift a finger."

"You won't have to," said Owen. "Thanks!"

"And put your dirty clothes in the hamper," Mrs. Foote shouted after him.

But Owen was already up the stairs and moving fast. Maybe two newts, he thought, pounding into the bathroom. One would be lonely.

Swish! He slam-dunked his shirt into the hamper. Sweating like a pig, am I?

He went and stood in front of the mirror. He looked at his dirty back over his shoulder in the mirror.

You'd better believe it.

8

THE LADDER OF SUCCESS

"You should have seen his face," said Owen. "He was so happy."

He opened the kitchen cabinet and took out three plates. "You know Joseph. He told his mom the truth about the snapping turtle and she made him get rid of it. He had the empty bowl still sitting in his room. He said he didn't want to throw it out. He put the new turtle right in it."

"Poor Joseph." Mrs. Foote put three forks on top of the plates. "That was a very nice thing you did, Owen," she called after him as he walked into the dining room. "I'm proud of you."

"Owen did something nice?" said Lydia. She

looked up from putting the glasses around the table. "Is he sick?"

"He bought a turtle for Joseph with the money Mr. White paid him for helping build the pond," said Mrs. Foote. She came and stood in the doorway with a bowl of spaghetti in her hands.

"Oh. That was nice," Lydia said. "Geeky, but nice."

"Lydia . . ." began Mrs. Foote.

"I'm only kidding," Lydia said. She grabbed Owen around the neck and started making fake kissing noises above his head. "Oh, Owen. Owen, my hero. You're so wonderful."

"Get off me!" Owen pushed her away and ran around to the other side of the table. "Peasant."

He put a hand on his chest and pointed his nose in the air, like royalty. "You're not worthy to kiss my shoes," he said.

"Who'd want to?" said Lydia. She sat down at her place. "Where's Dad?"

"At a faculty dinner." Mrs. Foote put the dish on the table and sat down. "He'll be home around nine."

Lydia grabbed the bowl and helped herself to the spaghetti. "How come you never buy *me* anything?" she said, pushing the dish toward Owen. "I thought charity began at home."

"No way," said Owen. "You have a lot more money than I do."

"That's because I save mine," said Lydia. "I have a savings account that pays me interest. You wouldn't know about things like that."

"That reminds me, Owen," said Mrs. Foote. "I read a very interesting article about allowances today."

"He's not ready yet, remember?" Lydia said.

"I am, too," said Owen. "I have two extra mouths to feed now. What did it say?"

"Well, it was written by a child psychologist," said his mom, "who recommends that parents pay children their allowance in one lump sum at the beginning of every month. That way, the child learns how to manage money better by having to spread it out over four weeks."

"Better yet," said Lydia, "the child only has to grovel once a month."

"Good idea," said Owen. He held out his hand. "That means you owe me twelve dollars, Mom. If I add that to the eight dollars I have left over from Mr. White, I'll have twenty dollars again."

"If we're going to do this, you have to do all the things we talked about, Owen," said Mrs. Foote. "And not only because you're getting an allowance, but because we all have to help out, right?"

"Okay, okay," said Owen.

"Now you can buy that fake throw-up you wanted for your birthday that's only ten months away," said Lydia.

"No way," said Owen. "I'm not wasting my money on stuff like that." He pulled his wallet out of his back pocket. "So where's my money?"

"So how's your bedroom?" said his mom.

They looked at each other across the table. His mom had a half-serious, half-amused expression on her face.

Owen knew what it meant. It meant she had

nothing to lose and everything to gain. She wasn't budging.

"Okay," he said. "But the minute I clean it, I get my money. I'm not kidding."

"No dirty underwear in the closet, and no piles of stuff you can't bear to part with all over the floor," said his mom. "I want you to be able to run a vacuum around that room without sucking up half your possessions. Do you understand?"

"Vacuum?" said Owen indignantly. "Who said anything about vacuuming?"

He thought about the marbles and paper clips he might use someday, the pieces of clay that were still a tiny bit soft, the bits of paper there was still a little room to write on, the broken pencils—all that valuable stuff on his floor, sucked up inside a vacuum cleaner.

"Owen . . ."

He heaved a huge sigh. His mom's voice told him he had reached the end of the line. "Geez . . ."

Upstairs, he threw himself across his bed and

looked into the tank on the bench against the wall. One of the newts was curled up under the piece of bark he had leaned up against the glass. The other one was half hidden by the moss.

Owen picked up the small notebook and the pencil lying on his pillow and wrote: "7:30 P.M. Socrates asleep under bark. Plato asleep under moss."

He chewed on the end of the pencil and waited.

"7:35 P.M. Socrates still asleep. Same with Plato."

"How's the room going?" his mom shouted up the stairs.

"Great!"

Owen got up off his bed and started to gather all the things scattered on his rug into a pile. He pulled a dirty sweatshirt from underneath the bed and put the pile on top of it.

He would probably have to buy a heat lamp, he thought, and a black light. Newts were nocturnal. If he wanted to observe them at night, he'd need a black light.

He grabbed the arms of the sweatshirt and

tied them together into a neat bundle. Then he looked around his room. Where to put it?

He crawled over to his dresser, pulled out the bottom drawer, and put the sweatshirt inside. Then he kicked the drawer closed and jumped back onto his bed.

And maybe one of those fountains, he thought, picking up his notebook. In case they wanted to go swimming . . .

———————

"I hear you're a working man." Owen felt his dad sit down on the edge of his bed. He opened his eyes.

"Did I wake you up?" said Mr. Foote.

"No. I was just thinking."

"Mom told me about the job you did with Mr. White," said his dad. "Congratulations."

"Thanks." Owen sat up. "Did you see my newts?"

He and his dad looked into the aquarium. The newts were nowhere to be seen.

"That's a good sign," said Owen. He lay back

down and pulled his covers up to his chin. "It means they've adjusted to their environment."

"It's nice being able to buy things with your own money, isn't it?" said Mr. Foote.

"It's great. Did Mom tell you I got a turtle for Joseph?"

"She did. That was a nice thing to do," said Mr. Foote.

"He was pretty happy," Owen said. "He's getting Kitty back, too."

"How come?"

"She was throwing up all over his grandmother's house. And his dad got an allergy test that showed he's more allergic to dust than cat hair."

"Good for Joseph," said his dad. "Tell me about the pond."

Owen told him all about it. "It was fun," he said at the end. "It was hard work, but it was fun."

"You've learned a valuable lesson," said his dad. "Work doesn't feel like work if you're doing something you love. Lots of people just want a job that pays a lot. But if you spend your life doing something you hate, all the money in the world won't make up for it."

"*All* the money might help," said Owen.

"You know what I mean." His dad crossed his legs the way he did when he was warming up to a subject. "It's more important to do something you love in life than it is to make money, Owen. Your job isn't just the way you make money, it's the way you live. Day in and day out.

"A wise man once said that most people spend their lives struggling to climb the ladder of success, only to find out when they reach the top that it's leaning against the wrong wall. Does that make any sense to you?"

Owen yawned. He knew his dad. If Owen showed any interest in what his dad was saying, he could go on lecturing him for hours.

So Owen yawned again and made his face go blank.

"I guess it's a little late for this kind of conversation," said his dad. "I'll let you get some sleep."

He stood up and walked over to Owen's

door. "By the way," he said, turning. "As nice as it is to be paid for working for other people, there's a pile of leaves still waiting for you in your own yard."

"Oh, yeah," said Owen. "I forgot."

"Well, don't forget tomorrow, okay?"

"Okay."

Owen listened to his dad going down the stairs. Then he rolled over onto his side.

He didn't know what his dad was making such a big deal about. It was simple.

If you could do something you loved for the rest of your life, you'd be happy. If you practiced it a lot and got to be really good at it, people would be willing to pay you.

That way, you could earn your living doing something you loved. And it wouldn't feel like work, it would feel like fun.

Except for raking leaves, Owen thought hazily as he drifted off to sleep.

He didn't care how good you got to be at raking leaves. It would always feel like work.